Christmas 1999

For Benny.
May the heavens hear
all your wishes.
I Love You! mama

From his home on the other side of the moon,
Father Time summoned his most trusted
storytellers to bring a message of hope to all
children. Their mission was to spread magical
tales throughout the world: tales that remind
us that we all belong to one family, one world;
that our hearts speak the same language,
no matter where we live or how
different we look or sound; and that we
each have the right to be loved, to be
nurtured, and to reach for a dream.

This is one of their stories.
Listen with your heart and share the magic.

For Sylvie and
her uncle Rick,
whose capacity
to love continues
to awaken
our hearts.

Special thanks to the talented artists who contributed their time and faith to these pages; to our Cedco Publishing champions Charles Ditlefsen, Mary Sullivan, Deborah Kamradt and Susan Ristow; and to the team of believers at Portofino Art Management, whose supreme dedication made this book possible, we offer our heartfelt applause.

The Star Gift

Inspired by a Grimm Fairy Tale

Flavia & Lisa Weedn

Illustrated by Flavia Weedn

Cedco Publishing Company • San Rafael, California

Once upon a time there lived a little girl who was all alone in the world and very poor. She had nowhere to live. All she had were the clothes she wore, a scarf, and one piece of bread.

She thought that if she walked through the forest, she might find a town on the other side. There, she hoped, she would meet someone who could help her find food and clothing, and a place to sleep in exchange for work.

So the little girl set out on a journey.

She had not gone far into the forest when she came upon a beggar. "Little girl," he said, "I am very hungry. Please give me your piece of bread, so that I do not starve."

The girl was very hungry, too, but because she was so kind and unselfish, she gave the man her piece of bread and kept on walking.

She walked for a very long time and began to grow tired, but she could not stop to rest because she was still in the forest and she knew it would soon be dark.

She met a woman who came to
her and said, "Little girl, my head is
so cold from the wind; please give me
your scarf to help keep me warm."

The little girl's head was cold from the wind,
too, but because she was so kind and unselfish, she
gave the woman her scarf and went on her way.

It was getting dark now, but the little girl kept on walking, in hopes of finding shelter for the night. Soon she came upon another child, a little boy.

He was shivering from the cold and said to the little girl, "I am very cold, and your jacket would keep me warm. Please, may I have it?" And although the little girl knew she might freeze without her jacket, she gave it to the little boy and continued on her journey.

By now it had grown very dark and very cold,
and the little girl was deep into the forest when
she met yet another child.

This child sat huddled against a tree, almost frozen from the cold. And when the poor little girl saw her, she said, "Here, I will give you my dress. It will help protect you from the cold."

She knew that if she gave her dress away, she would have only her apron to wear, but because she was so kind and unselfish, she gave her dress to the child and went on her way.

Seeing a glow in the distance, the little girl thought she had almost reached the town she had hoped for. But when she climbed up on a tree limb for a closer look, she saw it was only the moon shining down into the forest.

The poor little girl, too cold and weak
to go any further, sat down under the
tree, wrapped the apron around her, and
tried to cover herself with leaves. She
was colder and weaker than she had
ever been before.

Then the little girl began to cry
because she was so frightened and alone.
Through her tears she looked up into the
sky and wondered what would happen
to her. Seeing the beautiful stars, she
made a quiet wish and then fell asleep.

Suddenly the little girl was awakened when a star from the heavens fell from the sky . . . and then another and another.

The brilliant stars were falling down to earth all around her, and she quickly stood up, watching them in wonder.

The little girl began to catch the stars in her apron, until it overflowed with sparkling brilliance. And then, quite magically, the stars began to cast a bright light before her and embraced her with a cloak of warmth.

As the stars continued to fall, they created a pathway through the forest, and the little girl began to hear the faint sound of music in the distance. The stars moved forward, as if to guide her, and she followed their warmth and light.

As she walked, the music grew louder and louder, and soon there appeared before her a small house, with smoke rising from the chimney. She saw a family gathered on the porch playing music.

She walked toward the house, and just as
suddenly as the stars had appeared, they
vanished. Now, except for the light coming
from the house, the forest again was dark.

Before she could say a
word, the music stopped.
As she looked at the family,
she heard a tender voice
say, "Hello, little girl! Where
have you come from? You
look all alone and so cold
and hungry. We'd like to
welcome you to our home.
Please, come inside and
we shall feed you and keep
you warm."

The little girl could
hardly believe it, because
this is exactly what she had
wished for.

She entered the house,
and soon the little girl was
wrapped in a blanket, sitting
next to a warm fire, eating
muffins and drinking cider.
The family played beautiful
music for her, and she shared
with them her story of how
she had followed the starlight
and how it had led her to
their home.

She had no way of knowing that this family, too, had made a wish that night. They had wished for another child to join their family, a little girl just like her. Although they had not seen the path of light, nor twinkling stars, they knew this special little girl had been led to them for a reason . . . and that their wish was also coming true tonight. And because she was gentle, kind, and unselfish, the family loved her so much that they asked her to stay and live with them forever. With joy, the little girl agreed.

It was a most magical night for everyone, and happiness filled their home, but silently each of them wondered . . . Had the stars been watching this little girl from the night sky all along her journey? Had they witnessed her kind and giving nature, and had they really come down to Earth to help guide her way? Or had she simply dreamed it all?

The answer came later that night, as the family tucked the little girl into a warm bed. They wrapped a blanket around her, and the little girl felt something in her apron pocket. When she reached inside, a light filled the room, and out fell a hundred twinkling stars. Once again music filled the air, but this time it came from the sky above.

And then, with love in their hearts, they all thanked the heavens for what they had learned that day . . . that giving what you have brings love in return . . . and that somehow, someway, heaven always hears our every wish.

ISBN 0-7683-2054-2

Text by Flavia and Lisa Weedn
Illustrations by Flavia Weedn
© Weedn Family Trust
www.flavia.com
All rights reserved.

Published in 1998 by Cedco Publishing Company.
100 Pelican Way, San Rafael, California 94901
For a free catalog of other Cedco® products, please write
to the address above, or visit our website: www.cedco.com

Printed in Hong Kong

3 5 7 9 10 8 6 4 2

The artwork for each picture is
digitally mastered using acrylic on canvas.
This book is set in Journal Text.